For Iona

The Tale of the Turnip
is a traditional English tale retold by Brian Alderson

First published 1999 by Walker Books Ltd
87 Vauxhall Walk, London SE11 5HJ

Text © 1999 Brian Alderson
Illustrations © 1999 Fritz Wegner

2 4 6 8 10 9 7 5 3 1

Printed in Hong Kong

This book has been typeset in Opti Benson Italics.

British Library Cataloguing in Publication Data
A catalogue record for this book is available
from the British Library.

ISBN 0-7445-4910-8

The Tale of the Turnip

BRIAN ALDERSON *illustrated by* FRITZ WEGNER

WALKER BOOKS

AND SUBSIDIARIES

LONDON · BOSTON · SYDNEY

Once, a good time ago, there was an old farmer.
He lived in a ramshackle cottage, with a few chickens
and suchlike, and he looked after a few fields.

But just across the way there was an arrogant old squire, and he lived in a fancy great house, with stables and gardens, and fields and meadows, and chickens and pigs, and cows and horses, and who knows what else.

*N*ow one day the old farmer went
     out into his fields and planted a lot of turnips;

and some of them grew and some of them didn't.

But right bang in the middle of one field there was a turnip that grew ...

and grew ...

and grew ...

and grew ...

and grew.

"Hen's teeth!" said the old farmer to his missus. "This is a right champion turnip. We must take it to the king." So they got a block and tackle and they heaved it up, out of the ground and on to a wagon ...

and they took it to the king.

"*Stone the crows!*" said the king. "*That's the most champion turnip I ever did see.*"

He gave the old farmer a cart-load of gold
and the old farmer went home happy.

*W*hen the squire heard about this
he was furious. "What! – What! – What!" he shouted.
"Giving that old codger a cart-load of gold for a miserable turnip!
Why! I've got a stable full of horses out there, and any one of 'em's
worth a thousand turnips. I'll give the king one of those."

So he fetched out his best horse, put it in the wagon so as not to wear it out, and he took it to give to the king.

"*By gum!*" *said the king. "That's the most poshed-up horse I ever did see. Why – not even the crown jewels are a fit reward for a horse like that. What'll I give you? … I know … you can have …*

my champion turnip!"